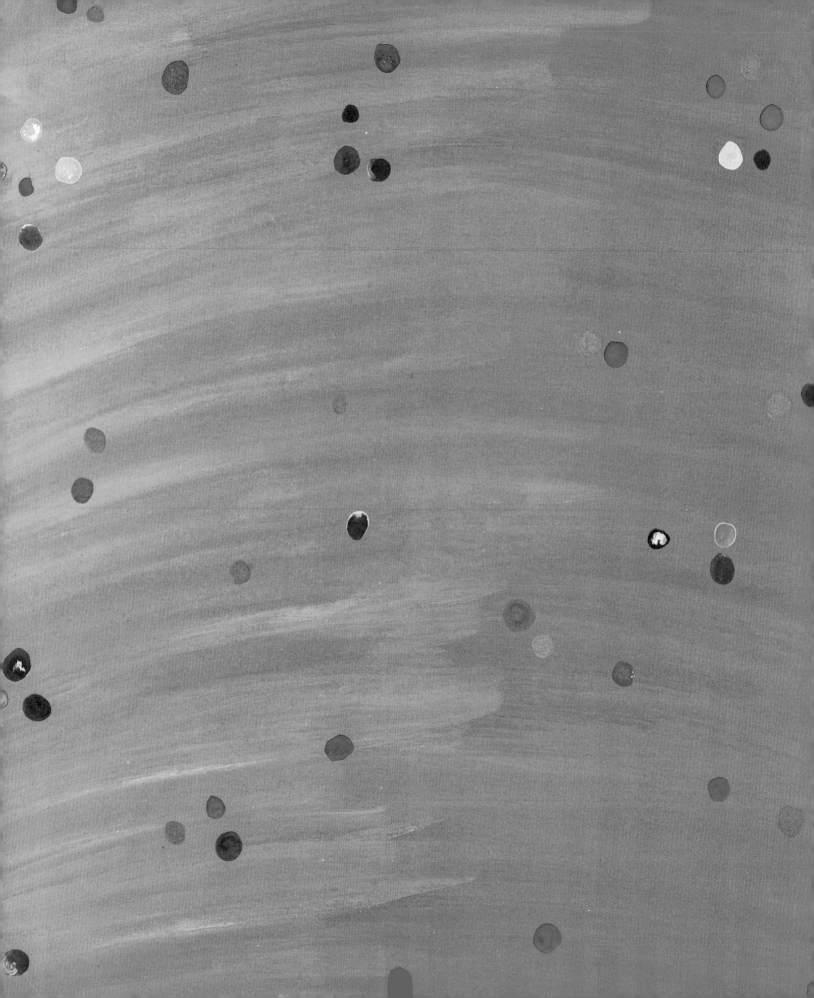

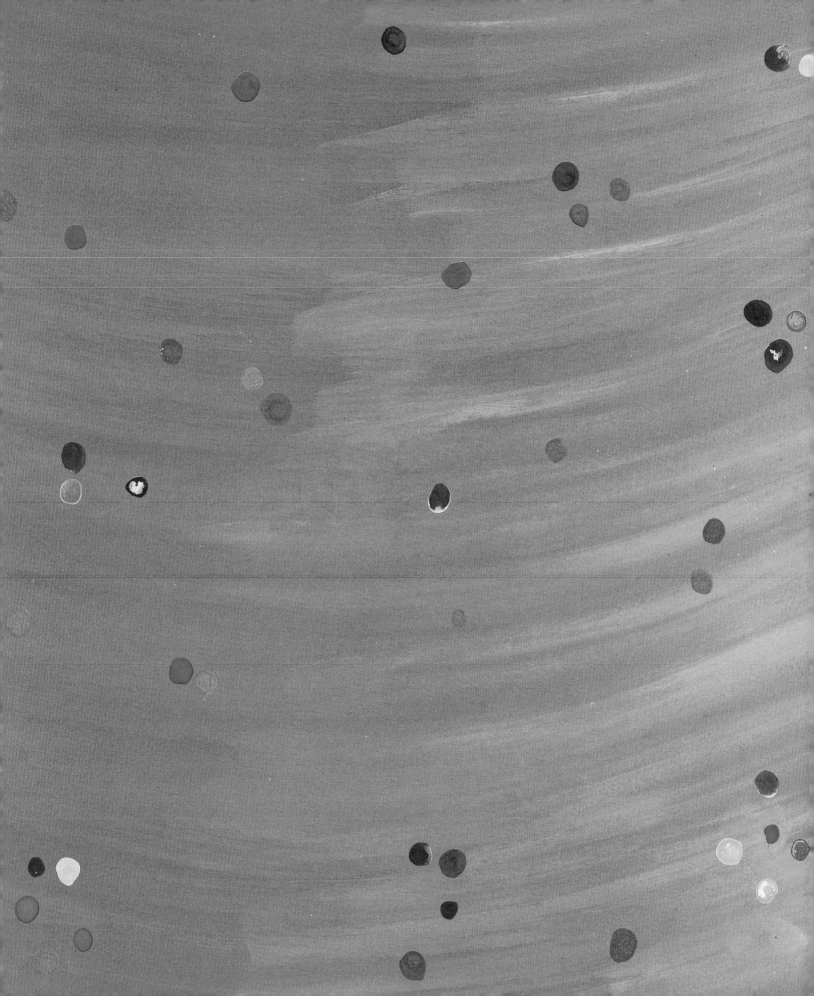

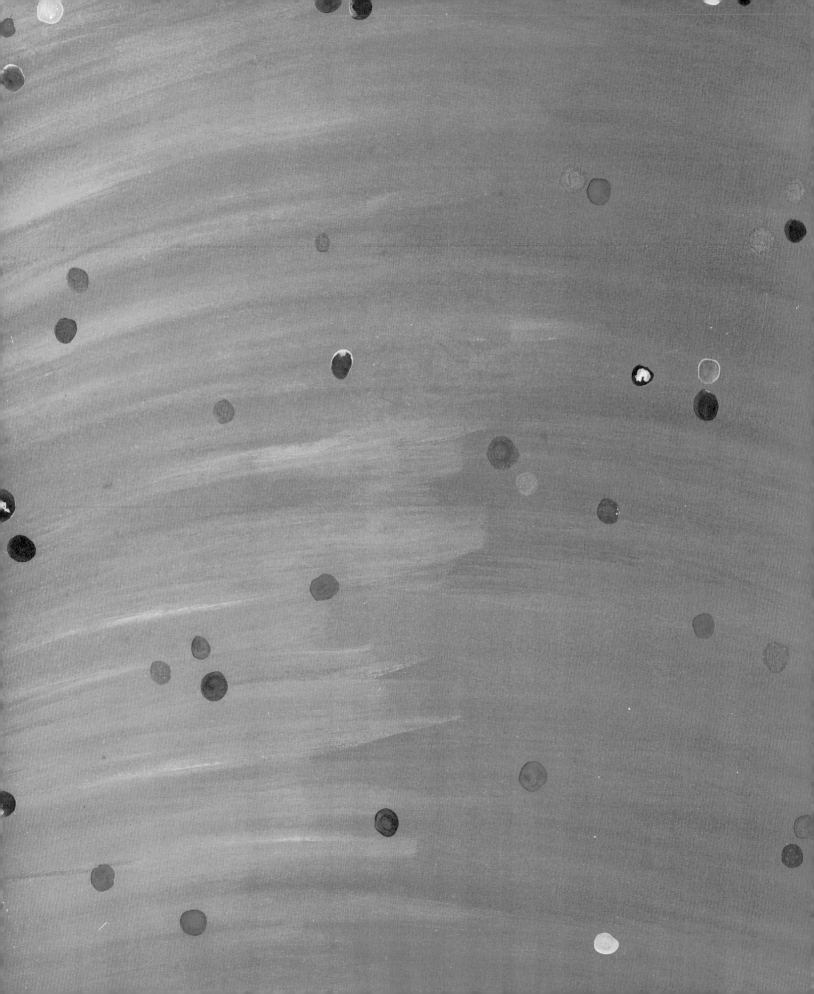

Vera B. Williams

"MORE MORE MORE," SAID THE BABY

3 LOVE STORIES

SCHOLASTIC INC.
New York Toronto London Auckland Sydney

This book consists of gouache paintings.
The lettering was done as part of the paintings
by the artist with the valuable assistance
of Savannah T. Etheredge.
It is based on Gill Sans Extra Bold.

ISBN 0-590-45198-7

Copyright © 1990 by Vera B. Williams.
All rights reserved. Published by Scholastic Inc., 730 Broadway,
New York, NY 10003, by arrangement with Greenwillow Books, a
division of William Morrow & Company, Inc.

12 11 10 9 8 7 6 5 4 3 2 1   1 2 3 4 5 6/9

Printed in the U.S.A.   08
First Scholastic printing, September 1991

For Hudson

For William

And for all our grandchildren

LITTLE GUY

This is Little Guy.

Little Guy runs away so fast

Little Guy's daddy
has to run like anything
Just to catch that baby up.

But Little Guy's daddy
catches that baby up all right.
He throws that baby high

and swings that baby all around.

"Oh you're a great little guy,"
Little Guy's daddy sings to Little Guy.

"Just look at you
with your perfect belly button

right in the middle
right in the middle
right in the middle
of your fat little belly."

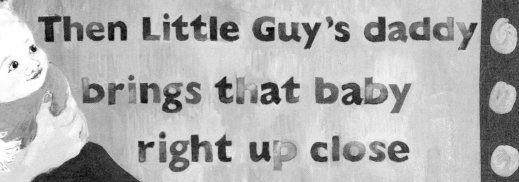

Then Little Guy's daddy
brings that baby
right up close

and gives that little guy's belly

a kiss right in the middle
of the belly button.

"More," laughs Little Guy.

"More. More. More."

Now this is Little Pumpkin.

Little Pumpkin scoots away so fast

Little Pumpkin's grandma
has to run like anything
just to catch that baby up.

But Little Pumpkin's grandma
catches that baby up all right.

She holds that baby nose to nose

and swings that baby all around.

"Oh my best little grandbaby,"
Little Pumpkin's grandma
sings to Little Pumpkin.

"Just look at you
with your ten little toes

right on the ends
right on the ends
right on the ends
of your two little feet
good enough to eat."

Then Little Pumpkin's grandma
brings that baby right up close

and tastes each
of Little Pumpkin's toes.

"More," laughs Little Pumpkin.
"More. More. More."

LITTLE BIRD

Now comes Little Bird.

Little Bird falls asleep so fast

Little Bird's mama
has to move like anything
just to catch that baby up.

But Little Bird's mama
lifts that baby in her arms all right.
She rocks that baby back and forth

and gets that baby ready for bed.

"Oh my best little baby,"
Little Bird's mama
sings to Little Bird.

"just look at you
with your two closed eyes

right on either side
right on either side
right on either side
of your neat little nose."

Then Little Bird's mama
brings that baby right up close.

She gives that little bird a kiss right on each of her little eyes.

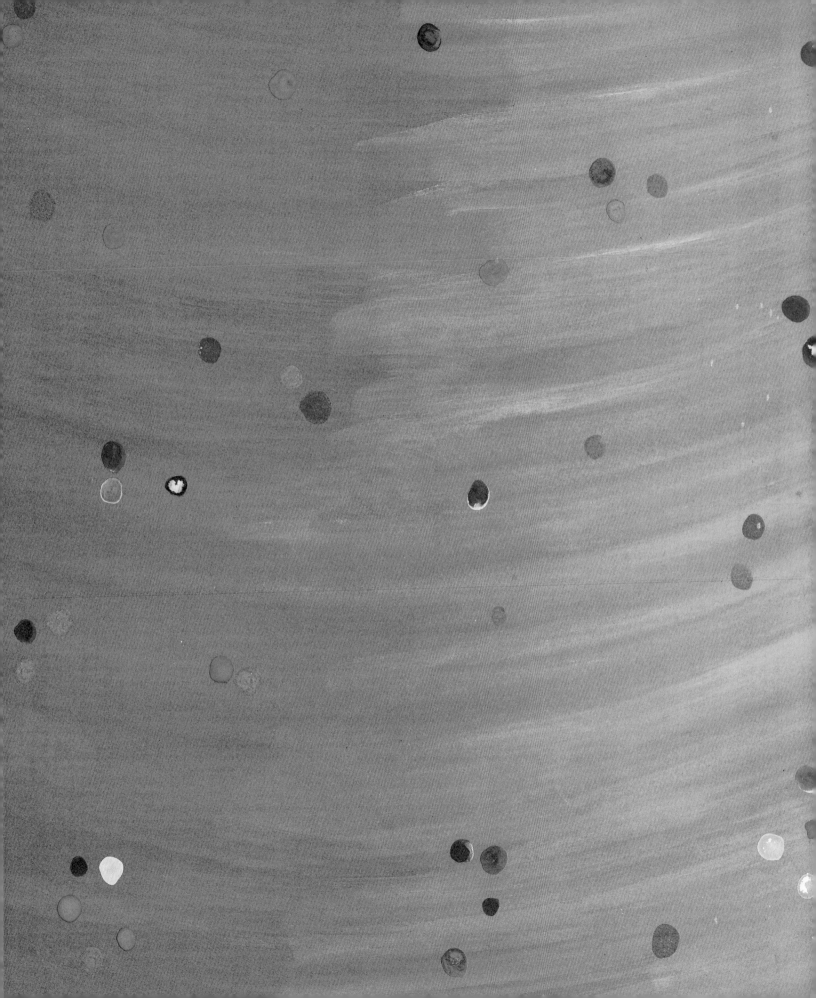

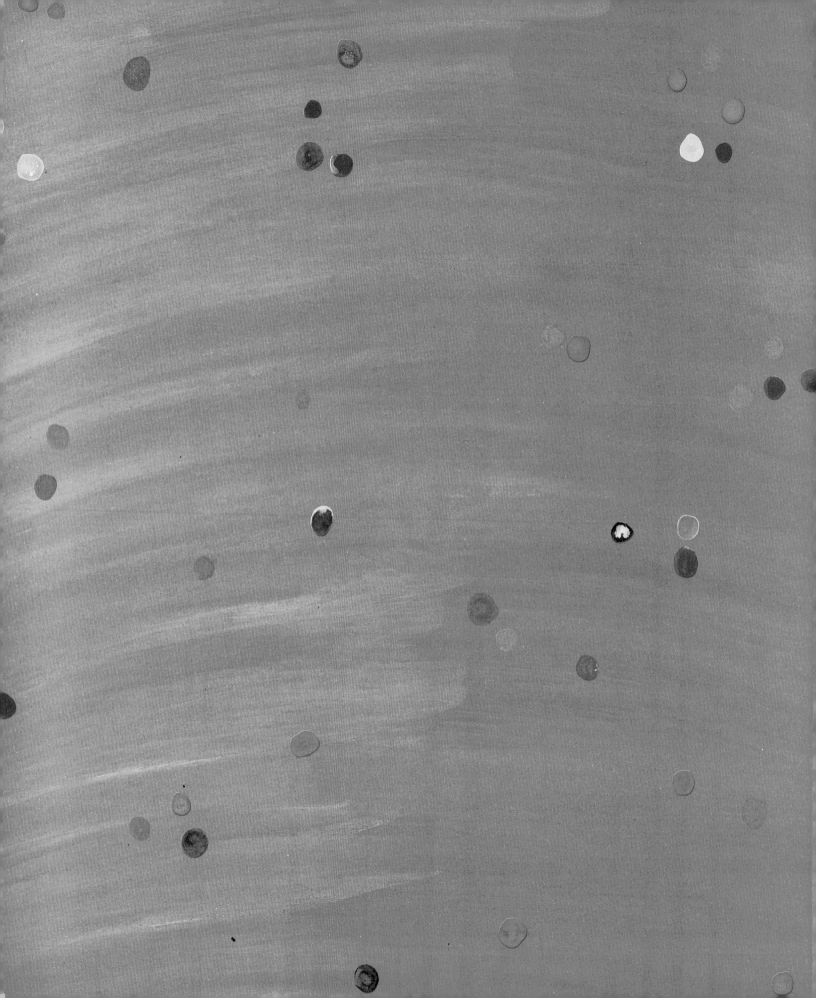